KALINE
KLATTERMASTER'S
TREE HOUSE

by

HAVEN KIMMEL

illustrated

by

PETER
BROWN

ATHENEUM BOOKS FOR YOUNG READERS
NEW YORK LONDON TORONTO SYDNEY

Acknowledgments

I would like to thank my editor, Caitlyn Dlouhy,
for her enduring faith and patience,
and brilliant editorial work.
Thank you to Christopher Schelling,
and most especially to
Scott Browning of the Hall Farm Center,
who gave me a miraculous gift.

ATHENEUM BOOKS FOR YOUNG READERS • An imprint of Simon & Schuster Children's Publishing Division • 1230 Avenue of the Americas, New York, NY 10020 • This book is a work of fiction. Any references to historical events, real people, or real locales are used fictitiously. Other names, characters, places, and incidents are products of the author's imagination, and any resemblance to actual events or locales or persons, living or dead, is entirely coincidental. • Text copyright © 2008 by Haven Kimmel • Illustrations copyright © 2008 by Peter Brown • All rights reserved, including the right of reproduction in whole or in part in any form. • ATHENEUM BOOKS FOR YOUNG READERS is a registered trademark of Simon & Schuster, Inc. • For information about special discounts for bulk purchases, please contact Simon & Schuster Special Sales at 1-866-506-1949 or business@simonandschuster.com. • The Simon & Schuster Speakers Bureau can bring authors to your live event. For more information or to book an event, contact the Simon & Schuster Speakers Bureau at 1-866-248-3049 or visit our website at www.simonspeakers.com. • Also available in a hardcover edition. • Book design by Krista Vossen • The text of this book is set in Edlund. • The illustrations are rendered in pencil and digital. • Manufactured in the United States of America • 0310 OFF • First paperback edition April 2010 • 10 9 8 7 6 5 4 3 2 1 • The Library of Congress has cataloged the hardcover edition as follows: Kimmel, Haven, 1965– • Kaline Klattermaster's tree house / Haven Kimmel ; illustrated by Peter Brown. — 1st ed. • p. cm. • Summary: Third-grader Kaline Klattermaster's father has gone somewhere and his mother cannot seem to keep everything straight the way he did, but the two brothers and one hundred dogs that live in his imaginary tree house—and his strange neighbor Mr. Osiris Putnaminski—help him cope with his father's absence, his mother's forgetfulness, and the bullies that torment him in school. • ISBN 978-0-689-87402-4 (hc) • [1. Divorce—Fiction. 2. Neighbors—Fiction. 3. Bullies—Fiction. 4. Schools—Fiction. 5. Imagination—Fiction.] I. Brown, Peter, 1979– ill. II. Title. • PZ7.K56483Kal 2008 • [Fic]—dc22 • 2007031979 • ISBN 978-0-689-87403-1 (pbk) • ISBN 978-1-4169-9915-7 (eBook)

This book is dedicated to my son,
Obadiah Kimmel,
whose imagination and sense of humor
are the great joys of my life,
and who lovingly shares his genius
with me every day.

And it is for a *certain someone*,
Orri Putnam.
If ever there were a hero
of grace and compassion
who happens to have the coolest
house in the world,
it is he.

PART ONE

DO NOT WALK ON GRASS!

DO NOT WALK ON GRASS!

DO NOT WALK ON GRASS!

DO NOT WALK ON GRASS!

DO NOT WALK ON GRASS!

DO NOT WALK ON GRASS!

DO NOT WALK ON GRASS!

DO NOT WALK ON GRASS!

Chapter One

DO NOT WALK ON GRASS!

On the last day of summer before third grade, Kaline Klattermaster, who was small for his age, sat on the top step of his front porch and looked around Hoppadoppalous Court. He made a grand waving gesture, since there was no one to see him do it. All of this, as far as the eye could see, had once been the domain of the noble warrior. OR, or maybe AND, it had once been so thick with trees that a squirrel could travel for miles from branch to branch without touching the ground. And there he was, the noble warrior heading down the road on a very friendly white horse—well, it was pony-sized and NOT scary, and the warrior was bringing Kaline gifts of feathers and . . . the other stuff they brought, like corn and beads! And there were squirrels, swinging from tree to tree, and they looked slightly like monkeys!

A car drove past and it was a loud car, and the warrior and the squirrels disappeared. TOO BADLY. Kaline squinted. And THEN sometime much later but he didn't know HOW MUCH later, all of this land, as far as Kaline's other eye could see, had been farmland, thousands of acres. And then TIME PASSED and all of the farms were sold, and these houses were built, including Kaline's own—EXCEPT for the house next door, the home of a *certain someone*. Kaline looked up and down the street, which was straight as a stick, at each square house on each square of land. He remembered for certain that all of his neighbors had $\frac{1}{4}$ acre of grass, or perhaps $\frac{2}{3}$, or even $\frac{25}{8}$ ths.

He was getting better with fractions. For instance, he understood that the slashy line in the middle went this way:—. Kaline hummed, scratched the top of his head, waved his arms above his head as if he were at a baseball game. HISTORY, however, was still a huge problem and who knew what was going to happen in the third grade. His parents had made a HUGE mistake by starting him in school a year early because of where his birthday fell, and also because he had been a WHIZ KID in day care. AHEM. It turned out that being the smartest BABY didn't matter all that much, did it? At the end of second grade he was asked what year our country had been founded and in his mind he saw the warriors, the trees, the flying squirrels, and he wrote: 1927. He looked at it. He changed it to 1289. Then suddenly he was overcome with the idea that there might be a year that began with "5," like "in the year 562," and he had to put his head down on his desk and pretend to snore.

Every house was the same EXCEPT for the one next door, which belonged to Kaline's life-long neighbor and *certain someone*, Mr. Osiris Putnaminski and his white terrier, Maestro. Mr. P.'s house was GIGANTIC and probably HAUNTED. A brick monstrosity is what his neighbor on the other side, Mrs. Jalopoly, called it. It was very old, built in 1827 or in 718, and Mr. P. still had FIVE acres of land, at least. He had his big yard, his flowering plants, and then at the back, beyond his garden, WOODS. They were his very own. He could swing from tree to tree there, should he desire.

Kaline tried marching without standing up. That worked. He tried to remember the words of "The Star-Spankled Banger," and he sang some of those. Could he wish Mr. P. out of his house with just the force of his mind? He tried, but the front door stayed closed. Eventually, Kaline knew, Mr. P. would emerge, a cane in one hand and a leash in the other, and he would walk the trotting white dog up and down the block. Mr. Putnaminski was a light-brown-skinned man with a beard and WHITE HAIR, which he wore in a PONYTAIL. Mrs. Jalopoly said it was scandalous, she said that between Mr. P.'s hair and beard and the belly he wore out in front of him he looked like a CRAZY SANTA CLAUS.

In addition to the house, the land, the woods, the dog, the ponytail, Mr. P. was in possession of an old car that moved through the neighborhood like a wild cat, but *slooow*, like a *very old panther*. He was retired from his former life as the owner of beauty schools, and he had a hobby that Kaline sometimes heard whispers of but he didn't know what it was, and as he looked down at his square of yard, which was bordered with yellow signs his father had planted that said: DO NOT WALK ON GRASS! DO NOT WALK ON GRASS! Kaline thought about his wishes in their order of wishedness:

1. He would like to get hold of that white dog and keep it.
2. He would like to explore those woods.
3. Don't talk to strangers was a problem, as this prevented him from engaging Mr. P. in the conversation that would lead to 1 and 2.
4. Was Mr. P. a stranger, or simply STRANGE?
5. He would like to roll around in the grass

and also DIG in it. The best thing would be to *peel up* the grass, dig around in the dirt for a long time, and then put the grass back down over the hole like A WIG, and then wait for someone to step on the hole.

6. But what if the dog fell in by mistake? Kaline would ONE HUNDRED PER-CENT not wish that; with all of his percentages he would keep the dog from stepping on the wig hole.

7. Some older brothers would be nice, also third graders like Kaline. P.S. At least one should have circus muscles and one should have a fast car.

8. He would like to know where his father was.

"So, Mr. Putnaminski," Kaline said, waving his hand at his neighbor's house. He was trying to look like a detective, so what that hand was doing swinging around like a conductor at an orchestra Kaline COULD NOT SAY. "You're a man of the world. When was the last time YOU saw my dad? And where have YOU been for the last two days? Or four? Do you know the last thing my dad said to me? 'Eat your green beans.' Last words. What do you make of that?"

Kaline scratched under his arms. In all the square yards around him no one appeared or moved or came out to offer him a surprise blackberry pie, so he gave up and stood up and brushed the dust off his pants. He opened the front door of his white house and slipped out of his shoes. Squinting through the dark living room, where the air conditioner was turned up so high the temperature was hovering around THREE, Kaline could see his mother sitting at the kitchen table, looking at the phone book and not moving. There was her

8

usual cup of coffee but she wasn't drinking it, and he thought maybe now was not the BEST TIME to suggest she make a pie, buy him a swimming pool, change her mind about video games, let him grow his hair out like Shaggy on *Scooby-Doo*, home-school him.

Kaline wondered: why was his mother just sitting like that? If his dad were here she would be *up to something*, and he would have to sigh and say "Estelle, Estelle," meaning why was she so scatterminded and dancing around the kitchen, why did she glue sequins and rhinestones to the frames of all of her eyeglasses, and *why* did she always have to ride her bicycle everywhere? A bicycle that was called by the name of 1977 Schwinn. Kaline had known its name since he was little. One Nine Seven Seven Schwinn was another way of saying it only his dad did not agree. Why did she take up candle-making and leave wax all over the kitchen, hmmm? Why learn the bongo drums? How did that help anyone, Kaline's father would have asked, and why weren't the drums put away neatly? Why the strange hats worn with the One Nine Seven Seven bicycle? Where were Estelle's shoes and why did they NOT MATCH, was another question often spoken out loud.

Kaline stared at his mother for one minute, or maybe an hour, but she didn't look up at him, so he went into his room, where his new backpack was already filled with school supplies, and next to it sat a grocery bag filled with paper towels and old socks for the dry-erase board and germ-killing hand goo. At the Super Humongnous Department Store, which seemed to Kaline the size of a small CITY, his mother had looked at the list of things he needed for the year, then sighed and said, "Soon they'll be asking us to buy shoes for the teachers," which Kaline didn't understand but for some reason found HILARIOUS. For the next twenty minutes or maybe it was eighty, he ran up and down the shoe aisle saying, "What about THESE? What if we provided these shoes for Mrs. Leetlemeyer? Or THESE? Can you picture these on Coach Joe, I ask you?" At one point Kaline had so exhausted himself with hilarity he had to lie down on the floor and his mother said, "Don't think I won't run over you with this cart," and he had started laughing again, and his mother had to stand him up MANUALLY and straighten his clothes. She said people were staring but they weren't, because everyone was taken up with a toddler in house slippers who was screaming so hard she was causing the other shoppers physical pain in their ears, including Kaline's ears. That had been two days ago, and where was his dad then? Was it that night with the green beans, or another?

Kaline took a running leap and jumped on his bed, causing it to crash against the wall. This happened every day. He waited for his mother to yell at him but she didn't. He picked up the stuffed husky dog he slept with at night, Banjo, and held him tight. For sure Kaline loved Banjo, even though his dad had said Banjo "wasn't real." This "real" statement had caused Kaline to stare at his dad with disbelief. Could his father not see that Banjo COULD NOT GET ANY REALER? The dog was *right there*.

Kaline held him tight—he could tell Banjo had that feeling again, the one that was like Empty— because Banjo really wanted a friend; he always had. But Kaline's dad didn't want other dogs in the house (too messy and noisy) and no other dogs had ever invited Banjo over to their doghouses to play, so he spent the whole day alone.

Kaline pretended to fall asleep, but fortunately was awakened by his pretend snoring. What a lousy way to spend the last day of summer THAT would have been!

Chapter Two

THE RULES OF DINNERTIME

The rules of dinnertime were very simple; they went something like this:

KALINE KLATTERMASTER:
1. You talk too much.
2. Put the imaginary bugle back in your pocket.
3. The chair is not a jungle gym.
4. How can you possibly move so much?
5. You are making us physically ill from dizziness.

6. We, your parents, beg of you some peace
   and quiet at the end of the day.

So Kaline had grown accustomed to not talking
at the dinner table, although all the not-talking he
did caused him to wiggle more, and thus make of his
chair more of a jungle gym. On one particularly bad
evening, he realized he was looking
at his father upside-down, Kaline
having somehow come to hang
on the chair like a bat. And
the macaroni and cheese that had
been IN his mouth came OUT
and landed on the floor with a
glop, and his dad left the table
to go out to the garage for Alone Time.

Kaline hummed one of his favorite songs from
when he was little, "The Mole People." He tried
just humming, but at the chorus some words

inadvertently popped out. "The mole people! They live in a hole, people!" He made a gesture he'd been making for as long as he could remember: He thrust his arm into the air as if carrying something grand. When he was much MUCH younger he would make this gesture and shout, "Long Live The King!" But tonight he didn't shout.

The kitchen table was a yellow rectangle and the kitchen floor was tiled with blue and white squares. Kaline knew that his dad preferred that the legs of the table line up with the squares of the floor in a certain way, and that the place mats be exactly two inches apart. Kaline got under the table and tried to line up the legs, but he couldn't remember where they were supposed to be, in the middle or on a line, and also the table was HEAVY AS A FULL-GROWN COW. So he focused on the place mats instead, but how to know two inches? Was that bigger or smaller than one foot or two ounces? If his dad didn't come home soon, here were the things that would soon become a problem:

1. The grass. All the grass, every little blade, belonged to Kaline's dad, and he spent many evenings and Saturdays and Sundays riding around on his tractor-mower, making sure nothing coming out of the dirt ever got longer than 1/tinyeth of an inch, and also that the lines the mower left were STRAIGHT.

2. The sprinkler, which came on at the same time every evening, ditto, Kaline had no idea of anything about making the sprinkler sprinkle.

3. The little yellow signs that kept the grass from being walked upon. These signs were—along with the tools in the

17

garage—the most important things to Kaline's dad. The most important things ON THIS PLANET WE CALL EARTH, and perhaps all other planets as well.

4. The alignment of such things as the table and floor, the place mats, the salt and pepper shakers, the shoes beside the door, the magazines on the coffee table, the socks in Kaline's sock drawer, the two cars—his mom's and his dad's—parked side by side. Kaline pressed his fingertips against his temples because the list of Things Lined Up Properly was very, very long.

5. Who would say, "Kaline, it is exactly 6:40 and I expect you to be downstairs in FIVE MINUTES for breakfast"?

6. Who would drive him to school every day, and sometimes be waiting with an umbrella if the weather was bad?

"Kaline, please stop spinning your fork that way."

"Was I spinning my fork?" Kaline looked down, saw his fork pointed east although he was sitting west. "What do you know."

He recalled the fine way he'd marched without standing up today, and did that. He glanced at his mother, who was looking out the window, and then as fast as he could he moved his peas around with the tip of his nose.

"Kaline!"

"I'm sorry! I had to."

Oh to do that again! But now his mother was watching him, hawk-eyed. If only he'd gotten his nose in the mashed potatoes, too. "The mole people! They live in a hole, people!"

Kaline's mother sighed, sat back in her chair.

"Did I sing that out loud?"

She had hardly eaten anything, but now she stood and took her plate to the sink, as if she were finished. She used to eat a lot and sometimes even hum while she ate, which would cause Kaline's father what he called DISTRESS.

"Can I have dessert?"

"You haven't eaten your dinner yet."

Kaline looked down, and it was true. He began eating as fast as possible, using his spoon as if it were the bucket of a steam shovel. When everything on his plate was gone, the hugest burp he'd ever made ACCIDENTALLY CAME OUT, and he tipped over and put his head down on the table with exhaustion. If his father were here he'd have been out the door a long time ago. Which reminded him.

"Just to ask you: Where is Dad?"

Kaline's mother was reaching for his plate, and she froze. She looked at him a moment, unfroze. "He's not here," she said, turning toward the sink.

Kaline threw his hands up in the air. He

wanted to say, "Duh, HELLO, I can see that." He wanted to say, "Duh, WHY DO YOU THINK I'M ASKING THE QUESTION, MISSY?" But both of those things were terrible rude and would have resulted in disaster, so he took the imaginary bugle out of his pocket, shined it up on his napkin, put it back without playing it. His mother gave him a strawberry Popsicle, told him not to dawdle because it was bath time. He could see that she had not forgotten about school tomorrow, even though he had carefully not mentioned it even once. Kaline wondered if he had missed Mr. P. and Maestro on their "constitutional," which is what Mrs. Jalopoly called it. This magical word applied to both Mr. P.'s evening walk AND The Declamation of Inkpendence, which Mr. P. had signed IN INK a long time ago. Kaline knew THAT much about history.

In the bathtub he fired his machine gun:

RAT-A-TAT-A-RAT-A-TATTA! He pretended to be a seal, a whale, a dolphin. Once in a while he would feel a nagging suspicion that A LOT of water was making its way out of the tub and onto the floor, and then he would forget. He sang all the Beatles songs he could remember, which was one, "I Want to Hold Your HAND." He was moving his hands toward his face and away, toward and away, trying to hypmotize himself, when he realized he was shriveled up like a RAISIN PERSON. "Ruh-roh, Shaggy!" he said, looking around for his dad's egg timer.

It was sitting on top of the cabinet and *no one had set it*. It was entirely possible Kaline had been in the bathtub *all night long*, and that he was now going to have to go school *soaking wet and wrinkled*.

"MOTHER!!!" Kaline called out. He waited for what seemed like ten minutes, then yelled again, "MOOOOOTTHHHHHEEE—"

"For heaven's sake," his mother said, opening the bathroom door, "what? What are you yelling about?"

"How long have I been in this bathtub?"

"I don't know," his mom said, as if such things didn't matter.

"I am SUPPOSED to be in the tub unsupervised for TWENTY MINUTES," Kaline began, gesturing to the heavens. "Then Dad comes in and washes my hair and says, 'Now hop out and brush your teeth.' He sets the TOOTH TIMER as well.

Two minutes for the top, two for the bottom."

"Are you done?"

"No. Then I get my pajamas on and Dad sets the READING TIMER and I am allowed to read in bed for FIFTEEN MINUTES. Where have you BEEN all my life??" Kaline was shocked, *shocked* at how little his mother knew about bath time.

"Look," his mother said, sitting on the edge of the tub, "how about we just, say, take the bath, brush the teeth, read some. No timer."

Kaline stared at her, speechless.

"You know, do those things for the amount of time it takes to do them and then stop."

He continued staring.

"These evening rituals were your dad's—he made those rules, and it was sort of his time of the day with you, so I went along with them. But since he's not here . . ."

"Look at these fingers! When he does get

home he will require garage time because of my monster skin!"

"I see."

"We can't just go INSANE. We can't allow our lives to become CHAOS and PANGEMONIA."

"Pandemonium."

"Will you PLEASE wash my hair now, before I wrinkle for permanent?"

"Did I hear you singing a Beatles song?" his mother asked, reaching for the shampoo.

"Yes! It goes like this," and Kaline started singing it at the top of his lungs. The best thing about songs was how you could forget the words—it hardly mattered! Because there were always new ones you could stick in where the old ones had been!

Chapter Three

BoTTOMS ON SEATs!

Well there was one thing for certain: Kaline's mother was NOT Kaline's father. In place of the "It is exactly 6:40 and I expect to see you downstairs in FIVE MINUTES for breakfast," came a frantic, "Oh no, Kaline, it's 7:15 if you don't get up right this second we're going to be late here's a chicken leg you can have it in the car! I overslept and passing the window I saw a glow outside and when I went out to see what it was I realized I left my headlights on or somehow they got turned on, at any rate, the battery is dead, it was an old battery anyway and my turning the key to try to start the engine seems to have not only killed *it* but something else, too, which is smoking as we speak! Hurry!"

Kaline scrambled out of bed, tripping over his comforter and sending Banjo flying into the air. He looked around frantically, thinking: school uniform, shoes, backpack, smoking car, chicken leg. CHICKEN LEG? What sort of person fed her son an old chicken leg in the car for BREAKFAST? AND WOULD THEY BE DRIVING THE CAR ON FIRE TO SCHOOL?!?

His school uniform was lying across his desk chair, but when he picked it up he realized that something very ODD had happened in the night, and his school uniform had gotten BIGGER while Kaline had stayed the same size. "MOOOOOOMM!" he yelled, then waited ten or twenty minutes. "MOOOOTTTTHHHEEEE—"

"Kaline, what?" his mother said, opening his

bedroom door. She had run up the stairs and was out of breath. "What are you yelling about?"

"I ask you!" he said, pointing to the khaki pants that folded themselves eight or nine times above his shoe, and the dark blue shirt whose sleeves hung nearly to his knees, as if he were an orangutan heading off for an education. "Who'd ya buy these for, SOME OTHER KID I DON'T KNOW ABOUT? Also, are you on fire anywhere?"

Kaline's mother studied him with a worried expression. "Oh dear," she said. "No, no, the car stopped smoking. However, I donated all your uniforms from last year to the recycling sale." She lifted the shoulders of the shirt, which hit Kaline at about his inner elbow, then lifted them the other way. "There's nothing to be done here. You're simply going to have to go as is."

"ALSO," Kaline said, his fists on his hips, "in the beginning of the year we're supposed to wear our khaki SHORT PANTS and the shirt with SHORT SLEEVES. Where are they, I wonder?"

Kaline's mother looked around, quite worried now. "I don't know! Your dad took care of all those things."

"You can say that again. But DON'T." Kaline blew out a little breath of disbelief. Took *care* of those things? "Because we are already late and I have come to see that our lives together are going to be ONE HUNDRED PERCENT PANGEMONIA."

"Pandemonium. And I'm trying, Kaline, I am. I'll meet you outside with your chicken leg. Go brush your teeth."

"Who will set the timer?!?" Kaline yelled, as his mother flew down to the kitchen. "And what is the dark meaning of this 'chicken leg' you keep speaking of?"

Kaline walked out of the house in his clown clothes

and made his way down the sidewalk, eyes toward the pavement. His mother appeared to be trying to fix the car. She had begun, Kaline could see, by spraying everything with the fire extinguisher, *and he had missed it*. Oh how he had longed—all of his life he had longed!—to take one of his dad's sixteen fire extinguishers, to hold the handle like Fireman Flip, Kaline's favorite action figger, to PULL THE PIN WHICH HIS DAD HAD SAID KALINE IF YOU EVER PULL ONE OF THESE PINS I WILL LOCK YOU IN YOUR BEDROOM UNTIL YOU ARE OLD, and then to point the white nose at something, *anything*, and SPRAY. He would have sprayed carefully, as if a fire extinguisher meant something, but was his mother a Future Firefighter for the American Way of Life? No, she was not!

"Mother! Did you use a legal and FFFAWL-approved fire extinguisher without reading the directions AT ALL? Did you spray it *willy-nilly*, because it appears you discharged the fire extinguisher in question WHILE SPINNING AROUND IN CIRCLES UNTIL YOUR EYEBALLS WERE WIGGLING. Is that what happened, hmmm?"

She didn't answer. The hood was up and she was pulling at wires and hoses randomly—wires and hoses that were covered with the *lifesaving white fluff of heroism*—and doing so with a piece of dead chicken in one hand. On the first day of school. Which meant that things could not possibly get worse.

Except they had, because some wild animal had stampeded in the night and bent all of his dad's DO NOT WALK ON GRASS! signs! Kaline dropped his book bag and tried to straighten them, because what if his dad showed up RIGHT NOW? He would think Kaline had done it! He would turn around and leave again. But how to know if they were *perfectly* straight? Wasn't that what telescopes were for?

"Kaline, stop dawdling!" his mom shouted. "We're taking my bike!"

No. No. Not the One Nine Seven Seven. "Where, Mother," Kaline began, "where do you intend for me to sit?" Oh how he feared the answer.

"In the basket! Come on!"

Just as Kaline was about to take off running, RUNNING ANYWHERE BUT TOWARD THE

BASKET, Mr. Putnaminski came out his front door with Maestro on his leash.

"Good morning, Estelle," he said, tipping his hat in her direction. "Going for a morning ride?"

"Osiris," Kaline's mother said, with her hand pressed against her forehead. "The car won't start and I was about to take Kaline to school in my basket."

Mr. P. nodded. "An adventure. I don't want to interrupt it, but perhaps I could take him to school, while you call someone about the car?"

"Oh," Kaline's mother looked around, as if lost. "Would you? It would help me so much."

WOULD YOU? Kaline stared at his mother with all of his eye strength. Were there *birds* in her brain? Was Mr. P. not a STRANGER? And as he stared, Mr. P. was turning around and heading toward his garage, to fetch the loony car, and it seemed no one was going to stop this DISASTER.

"Go!" his mom said, putting his book bag over his shoulders and forcing upon him the chicken leg. "Go now and you might make it on time! I'll see you after school, one way or the other."

He walked the distance to Mr. P.'s driveway, which was like 17 or 3 feet, and stopped before the gigantic panther car, which was running and in fact did sound like a growl now that Kaline was close to it. He glanced up, up at the crazy giant belly and white suit and hat made of hay or grass or whatever it was, all of it belonging to THE MAN HIMSELF.

Mr. P. bowed. "Kaline Klattermaster, I presume?" His voice was deep and BIG and had a very slight accent, as if his mouth had spun a globe and chosen a place at random.

Kaline looked down again.

"Your mother tells me you are in need of

transportation, and my heart soars like an eagle to make your acquaintance."

Kaline said nothing.

"Osiris, thank you so much," Kaline's mother called from under the hood.

"Estelle, always a pleasure." Mr. P. turned toward Kaline. "So, this is my neighbor lad. I believe I've seen you either dancing or having seizures on your porch for many years now."

Kaline thought, *Was I marching, or were those seizures?* How very interesting if they were. And what in fact was a seizure? He walked around to the passenger side of the (scary) wild beast (old) and climbed in. The seat was so big he felt like he was a figure from a dollhouse left on a normal-size couch.

Mr. P. climbed in and his side of the car sank a little. Even though he didn't want to, Kaline looked at the dashboard and the radio place and the glove box and all of it was like nothing he'd ever seen on a car before and in fact maybe this wasn't a car but some sort of science-fiction thing that would cause him to sprout weeds out of his skin or begin speaking in beeps. His chicken leg grew sticky in the fingers and so he started to eat it because he didn't know what else to do, and at exactly that moment Mr. P. backed out of the driveway with a slight burst of speed (very slight), just enough to send the chicken leg up Kaline's nose.

"What shall we discuss, young man? What is your favorite subject?"

Kaline looked out the window, thought about it. "My favorite subject is how school and other things keeps wastesing all my free time." He took another bite of chicken, and some dropped on his shirt, leaving a grease spot that would drive his father TO CRAZINESS. "That's all I'd like to say about it, please."

"I understand. Sometimes silence is our friend."
They drove the rest of the way without a word.

James Franklin Trippington Elementary School was
a consolidated county school, which meant that
kids came from all over the county, not just from
Kaline's neighborhood. There were three classes of
each grade, so the people you were with in the first
grade got scrambled up into a different combination
in the second, and a whole different one in the third.
They eventually all got to know one another was
the point, but for Kaline a more logical idea would
have been to put all the smaller, One-Year-Younger-
Than-Everyone-Else-and-Failing-at-Most-Subjects
students together where they would be able to hide
from the others and cling together like marmosets.

Take this year, for instance, when SOMEHOW,
against ALL LOGIC AND LUCK, Kaline had
ended up in class with three boys who were

gigantic, the biggest third graders he'd ever seen. One of them barely had any eyes, because they were buried under a shelf of forehead and a single eyebrow that lay across his brow like a sleeping caterpillar. Another was red-haired and had an eyetooth that stuck straight out like the tooth of a serpent. The third was dark-brown-skinned and was wearing a baseball cap with the number 0 on the front, which what the heck kind of team was called 0, but at any rate Kaline had assigned them names: Skracky for Mr. No Eyes; Devil Tooth for the red-haired boy; and Mr. Zero. Obviously.

Mrs. Gottlieb, their new teacher, had barely assigned their desks when she up and left the room—left the room FOR NO REASON KALINE COULD IMAGINE—and Skracky, Devil Tooth, and Mr. Zero were towering instantly over his desk like evil trees.

"What's this?"
Skracky asked,
roughing up
Kaline's hair.
"Do we have
Mr. Cowlick
Boy among us
this year?"

"And what is this?" Devil Tooth reached out and picked up Kaline's new compass and protractor, which he had specially chosen himself in teal blue. "I'll be taking these."

"I'm partial to the Digimon pencil bag myself," Mr. Zero said, slipping it off the desk before Kaline could make a movement of complaint.

Kaline looked straight ahead and prayed as he often prayed for the arrival of a superhero or at least a large dog, or his two older brothers who just happened to be third graders.

"Tell you what," Skracky said, leaning close to Kaline. "You bring us in some good stuff tomorrow and we won't break your ears off, how about it. Also we plan on stealing your pants."

The three boys had just taken their seats when Mrs. Gottlieb, MRS. USELESS GOTTLIEB, returned, flustered and with her arms around three paper bags. "I'm going to need you kids to help me count these rolls of toilet paper, so get in a circle on the floor."

Kaline ended up sitting next to a girl with hair so pale it might have been cotton fluff from the County Fair. She wheezed when she talked, and she wore glasses. Her name turned out to be Georgia, and she moved so slowly Kaline began to wonder if maybe she was stuck on a slow-motion button, and if perhaps he should try to find the one that made her move normally.

"I hate those boys," she leaned over and whispered

to Kaline. "Those three. For some reason the school keeps letting them stay in the same class. My mom says it's because their parents 'put up a big stink' is how she says it, so they won't be separated. Last year they tore the head off my baby doll and left it in the drinking fountain, so I would find it after recess. I took to screaming and had to go to the principal's office, but not one thing was done about them."

Kaline sighed. "So I have no hope."

Georgia sat back and slowly finished counting her four rolls of toilet paper. "Nope. Not really."

The rules of third grade were REMARKABLY like those of second! Kaline was astonished! They went like this.

KALINE KLATTERMASTER:

1. Please do not toot unto the imaginary bugle.

2. Do not repeatedly kick the metal bottom of your desk, lest you shall be sent to the hallway.

3. Bottom on your seat! Bottom on your seat!

4. Neither is your water bottle a bugle, nor is it a trombone.

5. Try to write consistently with one hand. If that's your left hand, fine. If it's your right, even better. But don't move the pencil back and forth from one hand to the other, when what you have produced with either hand is illegible.

6. Sitting under your desk is forbidden, as is sneaking out to the hallway to stare at the art on the bulletin board. If I continue to glance up and find you missing, I shall be forced to call the police.

7. Christmas carols are lovely, especially at Christmastime. Do not hum them during

math, nor should you accidentally shout their choruses aloud and then ask, "Did I just do that?" YOU DID.

So far on that first day Kaline had been asked to copy some sentences out of his social studies book on the arrival of Christopher Columbus, and in the time allotted had gotten as far as writing his name, and the date, which he recounted as 27 Anguish 2096. That was it. The other students had written whole BOOKS about this Mr. Columbus, they were DOCTORS OF KNOWLEDGE concerning Mr. Columbus. Where had the time gone? Kaline looked down at his pad and saw that in addition to his name, he had managed to make 7,891 pencil marks all around the edge of the pad. Straight little lines. As if the page and the sentences it was intended to contain were a PRISON.

Kaline marched in place, slipped his bugle out of his pocket and gave it two short toots, which was all he dared. He managed to make them sound like the faraway cry of the heart-sore Canada goose, and so everyone looked out the window and not at him, and HMMMMM, Kaline thought, I wonder if I have a future in this noise-making.

Well, FOR ONE THING, he imagined telling someone, I AM HAVING A VERY DIFFIMULT DAY. If he tried to make a list of all the problems he needed to solve just to keep his life in order he would be in the third grade for many, many years, given how long it took him to write the simplest thing. So he said them in his head and held out fingers for their numbers.

1. Where exactly is my father?
2. How to get out of this third-grade class-room, where my life is at risk from boys

who are twenty-five years old, or maybe even twelve?

3. Chicken legs for breakfast. It is wrong.

4. How to keep the information out of the wrong hands—the fact that while all of his classmates were eight and heading toward nine, Kaline had only turned seven TWO WEEKS AGO AND THUS WAS A HAIR AWAY FROM SIX YEARS OLD. Six years old! However, if asked he was prepared to say he was seven as if he had been seven all his life, because he WAS seven and six was now SO FAR AWAY he could barely remember it—he might as well have never BEEN six.

5. He had been ordered into the vehicle and into talking with Mr. P. (stranger + strange), when what he wanted more than anything was to be taken to school at

PRECISELY THE RIGHT MOMENT in his father's car where there wasn't a speck of dust and everything was on time.

By the end of the day Kaline had failed to complete a single math problem, he had been unable to read the beginning of his Boxcar Children assigned book, because every time he read a sentence he saw it too clearly in his mind and then he had to just GO THERE and periodically make SHOUTING SOUNDS, and once he ended up with his nose against the blackboard, and once in the actual closet where in the winter their coats would hang. When the last bell rang, Kaline gathered up his things with a weary sigh. Every day. Day after day was going to be just like this.

That night, late into the darkness, so late it was almost EARLY, Kaline had a dream that the Giant

Whoppy-Jawed Hoodlums of his third-grade class-room were outside his bedroom window, trying to get it open. Banjo was barking at them with his most ferocious bark, but they kept at it, prying at the corners of the screen and trying to slip their sausage-fat fingers under the edge of the frame. That's all there was in the dream, just Kaline cowering in his bed, the window, Banjo barking, but somehow it was all so terrifying that Kaline sat straight up in bed, breathing hard. He was sweating, and his hair was stuck to his forehead. He decided to go get into bed with his parents.

He was halfway down the hallway when he stopped, realizing AGAIN that his dad was gone and WHERE WAS HE? Kaline sighed, exhausted. He could barely keep his eyes open, barely think straight. *Oh, well*, he thought, *I'll get in bed with Mom and I'll just have more room.*

Kaline knocked on her door but his mom didn't

hear him. He knocked again, but was too tired to wait for an invitation.

"Mom?" he whispered. The room was dark, and he couldn't hear a sound, no breathing, no movement of the blankets. "MOM?" Nothing. Kaline flipped the light switch on and saw the bed had no people in it and was still neatly made from this morning. "Ooooookay," he said, backing into the hallway. "Ummmmmm, MOM?" She wasn't in the bathroom. He ran the length of the house into the kitchen, sliding on the floor in his sleeping socks. His dad worried that Kaline would Catch A Deadly Cold if he didn't sleep in socks, and oh by the way WHERE WAS HIS DAD AND WHERE WAS HIS MOTHER?

"Mom?" Why was he speaking softly when he meant to be yelling?

Not in the living room, not in the coat closet, not under the couch. Not under the towels in the linen closet, not in the microwave. Maybe they had crossed paths, or else she hadn't caught up with him yet! He started over in his own room. Not there. Walked toward his parents' room, now really QUITE frightened, saying "Mom? Mom? Mom?" but she STILL wasn't in her bed, and by the time he slid into the kitchen for the second or eight-teeth time and there was no sign of her BUT SUDDENLY HE COULD HEAR SOMETHING ON THE ROOF, SOMETHING TRYING TO GET INTO THE HOUSE, he knew he should pick up the phone but he couldn't for the life of him remember the three numbers he was supposed to dial, what were they in which order, and obviously this was an extraterrestrium situation and the phone wouldn't work even if he knew the numbers WHICH HE DID NOT.

Without thinking about it, and he would be the first to admit he really wasn't thinking straight as an arrow about anything, he went flying out the front door screaming AAAAAAAAAAAAA! still in his pajamas and sleeping socks, his arms flapping around like a chicken, WHY? WHY KALINE WHY ARE YOUR ARMS FLAPPING ABOUT SO? He ran down the sidewalk, he DID NOT WALK ON GRASS! and across the driveway and right up onto the porch of Osiris Putnaminski. Kaline pounded on the door screaming AAAAAAAAAAAAA! and Maestro on the other side of the door was barking so hard and with such a pleasing little rhythm he sounded like a snare drum: BARKBARKBARK! [Very tinetiest pause.] BARKBARKBARK! [Pause.] BARKBARKBARK!

The door swung open. "Mr. Klattermaster?" Mr. P. was wearing fancy pajamas under a fancy robe and he wasn't wearing his hat, which looked a little odd at first, but then Kaline thought it would have seemed MUCH odder if Mr. P. slept in his hat, as Kaline's mother sometimes—

"MY MOTHER!!!!!! AAAAAAAAAAA!!"

"All right then." Mr. P. was very calm. He stepped onto the porch and closed the door on Maestro's frantic drumbeats. He gathered Kaline against him, that was the only way Kaline could think of it, he gathered him up, all the while saying, "Let's go to your house, tell me what the problem is, take a deep breath, here is a handkerchief, you'll find as you grow older that a gentleman always carries a handkerchief," and Kaline, now hiccuping, was able to say, "MY MOTHER HAS GONE MISSING JUST LIKE MY DAD AND WE ARE GOING TO NEED TO CALL THOSE THREE NUMBERS TO MAKE THE POLICE COME BUT I FORGET THE ORDER OF THE NUMBERS, oh, and also do you think we could get their pictures printed on milk cartons? I imagine it would be very helpful, and maybe we could also make some posters to hang in the neighborhood."

They were almost to Kaline's house; they were heading up the front walk when Kaline's mother came running out of the house screaming AAAAAAAAAAAA! She saw Mr. P. and shouted, "Kaline isn't in his bed and the front door was standing wide open!"

She was, Kaline's dad would say, an in-ex*cusable* MESS. Her green and blue knitted cap was covered with cobwebs and dust bunnies; there was even a stray feather sticking out of it. Her glasses were sitting catty-whompus on her face, and she was in her favorite pajamas, the blue ones with the white puffy clouds, EXCEPT she was wearing bib overalls ON TOP OF THEM, as if someone at school was threatening to take the top layer of *her* clothing!

"You are an in-ex-cusable mess, Mother."

"AAAAAAAAA! Kaline!!!!" She tripped over her own gardening shoes running toward Kaline and Mr. P., and then she had her arms around them. With Mr. P.'s humongnous arm around Kaline's back, and his mom's whole entire HUMAN PERSON swallowing him on every other side, Kaline was forced to say, in a very flat voice like someone who had been hit by a steamroller, _{"Helllo? A little air in here?"}

Oh no, and then she was KISSING them both. She was saying, "Osiris, thank you thank you," as she kissed him on the cheek, and to Kaline, "Thank heavens you're all right, thank heavens," AS SHE KISSED HIS WHOLE HEAD.

"I did nothing, Estelle," Mr. P. said, shrugging

his shoulders. "I merely answered the door when the lad threw himself against it, screeching like an angry chimpanzee."

Is that *what I sounded like?* Kaline squinted, trying to remember. How incredibly cool, if so.

"Now." Mr. P. moved Kaline toward his mother, using just the tips of his fingers, "I imagine the two of you will want to have some sort of reunion, so I'll leave you to it. But for good measure, why don't I just stand here on the sidewalk until you're safely in the house and I've heard the locks turn?"

Kaline's mother tried to straighten herself up. She adjusted her hat (making it more crooked) and moved her glasses a bit (less crooked) and pressed her fingertips against her cheeks (meaning she was feeling shy). "Oh, you don't need to do that. We'll be fine. But it's very kind of you to offer." She took Kaline by the hand. "What were you doing, out running around at midnight?!?

What were you thinking? What if Mr. P. hadn't found you??" She said this last part as if she might begin crying.

"Now HOLD YOUR HORSES, COWBOY ESTELLE. For the record, and I would like this written down somewhere so I can bring it up again if I ever get in really bad trouble, for the record, I HAD A VERY BADLY TERRIFYING DREAM, and I came to your bedroom NOT TO GET IN BED WITH YOU, *NOT*, but just in order to be sure you weren't having one too," he said as they walked up the steps, "and YOU WERE GONE COULD YOU PLEASE EXPLAIN THAT???"

Kaline's mom held open the screen door, waved Kaline inside. "I was in the attic, looking for yarn, for your information. In the future, I'll either ask for your permission or leave notes all over the house telling you my location. I'M IN THE DINING ROOM. WHOOPS, NOW I'VE

MOVED TO THE KITCHEN." She locked the screen, started to close and lock the storm door.

There was a second, a little bit of time, for Kaline to look outside, to the place he'd come from. Mr. Putnaminski was standing at the end of the front walk, just as he said he would be, waiting for their locks to turn. He had his arms crossed and looked very patient and comfortable, and as if he could stand there all night, if need be. Mr. P. saw Kaline and tipped an imaginary hat to him. Then the door was closed, and the locks were being turned. Kaline was about to say, "Let's invite him in for hot chocolate, to thank him," but his mom was stomping off down the hallway.

"HAVE STEPPED INTO PANTRY TO GET YOU A SNACK. OKAY, AM BACK FROM THERE."

Kaline shook his head, followed his mom down the hallway. He made a little circle around his temple with his fingertip: *cuckoo*. But he stopped VERY FAST when his mom turned around and almost caught him. "I was just waving at you," he said. His mom shook *her* head at *him*, turned back around. She made a little circle around her temple with her fingertip.

"I SAW YOU DO THAT," Kaline said.

"I was just waving at you," his mom replied.

Chapter Four

CHAOS AND PANGEMONIUM

When Kaline told his mother he needed to replace his protractor, compass, and pencil bag, she asked why and he said, "Because three grown men took them from me at school yesterday. Also they are extorting me for even more interesting things or they will break off my ears."

"Really? Are these men in any way related to the aliens that appeared in your room and cut star-shaped holes in your curtains?"

"No, these are different men. But one of them is similar to the aliens."

"Do they have hovercrafts, speak in a beeping language?"

"Not that I've noticed."

"Aaaand they're for sure not the super-tall cowboys who eat all the cookies and drink milk directly from the carton, leaving puddles on the kitchen floor?"

Kaline said, "They are NOTHING like those huge cowboys. And the cowboys also ate all the string cheese and a cherry Chapstick, just to tell you."

His mother sighed, having just returned from her office job. He could tell she wanted to take off her shoes and knit as she watched television for an hour or so, but instead she said, "Get in the car." So they got in the rental car his mom was using until hers was fixed, and Kaline grabbed a Pop-Tart to take with them as a snack, and as they backed out of the driveway Kaline's mom accelerated so quickly Kaline bonked his head on the dashboard and Pop-Tart went up his nose. "Oh, and also we need three more boxes of tissues for the classroom."

His mother was very bigly unspeaking.

"And apparently they will be taking my pants."

When they arrived home, Kaline's mom *accidentally* pulled in the driveway too close to the edge of the yard and ran over seventeen of the DO NOT WALK ON GRASS! signs. "Oh no!" Kaline said, jumping out of the car.

"Help me carry these things in," his mom said. "Your aliens stole the originals, after all."

"Leave them, I'll carry them in in just a second." Kaline pretended to be very busy inspecting the bark on the little maple tree his dad had planted last spring, and which didn't appear to want to grow. It didn't have any bark; it was more like a pencil with some leaves. As soon as his mom was

inside, Kaline rushed over to the signs. He realized he was actually MUTTERING OUT LOUD
like one of the old men in front of the tattoo par-
lor downtown, *I've got to get these fixed before he
gets home, how straight is straight enough?* when a
LARGE SHADOW with its LARGE BELLY fell
over him.

"Mr. Klattermaster?" Osiris Putnaminski was
standing before him, and Maestro was sitting,
looking interested. "Do you need some help?"

Now where had HE come from, and so quietly?
Was he perhaps a relation of the noble warrior,
who as everyone knew could walk over crunchy
things like potato chips without making a sound?

"That's okay," Kaline said, pulling up a sign
and trying to drive it back into the ground the
way his dad would have. Maybe he *should* invite
Mr. P. to help? Which thing—*yes, help me* or *no,
don't help me*—was the more ruder?

Mr. P. knelt beside him. "Do you know what my father used to say about big jobs like this?"

Kaline looked at him. "No." Well, HOW COULD HE? Kaline didn't even know the man, let alone his FATHER.

"He would say, 'Every hand helps.' And I've got two, so shall I?" For a big man, Mr. P. was up and down pretty quick. Before Kaline knew what was happening, the two of them were brushing off the runned-over signs and putting them back straight as could be.

"My dad says A Place For Everything And Everything In Its Place," Kaline told Mr. P., sort of without meaning to.

"Yes, I've heard that phrase. Do you think he's right?"

"Well, duh," Kaline said, then as fast as he could, "*excuse me* for the terrible rude. I absolutely believe it 100 percent! Look around! Where would we be if that tree just decided to up and get on top of your car is but one example! Trees go there, shoes by the door, table on the four corners of the . . . something, salt shakers, place mats two inches apart. Otherwise?"

Mr. P. wiped a sign DIRECTLY ON HIS PANTS. "Chaos?"

"Yes sir," Kaline said. "You said that right."

"Things would be crazy."

"AB-SO-lutely." He hesitated. For Kaline, sometimes the Leading Up to Saying Something was

much much worse and harder than the Finally
Saying It. He was in the Leading Up To part and
thought his brain would explode. *Just say it just say
it just say it*, aaargh! Yuck! Ptewy! He hated this!!
He didn't want to say it he didn't want to he didn't
want to he "You were nice to help me and my
mom last night, I'm sorry she's bonkers."

Mr. P. said, "Truly, I did nothing. I merely
answered the door when you knocked. And
Estelle is not bonkers."

She isn't? "She's not?"

"Heavens no. She's delightful, a treasure. She
marches to her own drummer, if you know what
that means."

"At my school the teachers say You March To
Your Own Drummer when they mean You Are
Weird."

Mr. P. sat back and laughed. LOUDLY. Kaline
hadn't meant to be funny, but then he heard

himself saying You Are Weird and *he* started laughing, and Mr. P. was wiping his eyes with his hankychief, and Kaline had to lie flat down on the driveway. Maestro strolled over and sat down next to him. The dog studied Kaline; he cocked his head a little to the right, and the look on Maestro's face seemed to say, "Marching to your own drummer, huh?" Which Kaline accidentally said out loud, the whole thing, and Mr. P. had to find his emergency hanky, while Kaline rolled around in the driveway, getting rocks in his hair.

At dinner that night Kaline lay on his stomach on his kitchen chair, arms outstretched like an airplane. He made airplane noises. His mother pretended not to notice. At one point his left wing accidentally grazed his plate and seventeen corns fell off onto the table, and still no one left and headed out to the garage.

"Ummm, Mrs. Klattermaster?" Kaline said. "I fear to tell that I have just spilled corn on the table."

"Then pick it up," she said, getting herself another glass of iced tea.

Kaline picked up each tinety kernel one at a time and thought HMMMMM. Perhaps she is ill, for it seems she cannot see what I am doing, in addition to how she was not doing her usual singing and dancing and wearing of odd hats. He tried using his knife as a backhoe, pushing his potatoes into a heap as if at a landfill, and then his spoon as that steam-shovel bucket, wherein he dropped a load of peas on top, and still his mother sat at her place, eating quietly and looking at the paper. The backhoe MEEP MEEP MEEP-ed as it reversed, so as not to run down any innocent bystanders or dogs or escaped felons. The steam shovel made a CRRRRRKK sound as it moved across to the corn, down to scoop, and up again. What was called for here was a cherry picker, OBVIOUSLY. Something he could ride in and supervise the whole operation while also messing about dangerously with the town's electrical lines.

"Just to ask you: Do you where my dad is?" Kaline asked it out of the blue, trying to trick her into answering.

She turned the page of the paper, didn't even glance up. "He's not here," she said.

"Can I have dessert?"

"You didn't eat any of your dinner."

Kaline looked down and was STUNNED to find it was true. He turned the shovel toward his own face, burped like some prehistoric monster, tipped over, and put his head down on the table. The only thing that kept him from passing out completely was playing "Taps" on his bugle, and the fact that his mother slipped a grape Popsicle under his arms, and he ate it still lying down.

Homework time consisted of:

1. Fill out your emergency contact form. He knew he should give it to his mother, but what would she say? His father had always been one of his two emergency contacts, and also he was far better in emergency room–type situations. With his father missing, what if she used Mr. Osiris Putnaminski? He obviously WAS their Emergency Person, but if Mr. P. ever came to Kaline's school, everyone at the James Franklin Trippington Elementary School would see an INSANE-LOOKING SANTA CLAUS NEIGHBOR WITH PONYTAIL. They wouldn't understand him *at all*. Kaline slipped the card under his mattress.

2. **Tell Us About You!** Kaline was supposed to list his name, his age, his hobbies, his pets.

He was expected to do this, he presumed, WITH A PENCIL, which was one of his least favorite pieces of wood on Earth. He preferred the sad little maple tree outside.

He looked at the form a long time, trying to figure out if he could list Banjo as a pet without danger, when he was compelled to jump on the bed and roll around and around, pretending he was rolling down a snowy hill. No hills where Kaline lived, unfortunately. Then he realized: he could not move. "HELP!" He yelled, but the sound was muffled! "HELP I AM COCOONED IN A PRISON OF MY OWN MAKING!!" Nothing. "MOTHER! MOOOOTTTHHHHEEER!"

His bedroom door opened. "Whaaaat? What is it this time?"

"Could you kindly remove me from this python of bedding?" Kaline asked quietly.

"Could you try rolling the opposite way you began?"

And that was pretty much it for homework. His father would have sat with him at his desk and made Kaline do it and he would have said, "Will you hold the pencil if I make it very, very sharp?"

At bath time Kaline set the egg timer himself, but for the life of him he couldn't figure out if he'd set it for twenty minutes or two hundred, and there was that old problem again of shrivel up, soak all night, go to school in raisin form, and suffer more humiliations and thefts. Finally he trusted he understood what was twenty and got into the bath and there followed explosive behavior from his machine gun, splashing of water on to the walls and floor, and a rousing rendition of "The Wheels on the Bus," which was not grown-up enough a song for the likes of him but it sounded good in the tub.

His mother didn't come when the timer went off, so hours passed, and finally Kaline washed his own hair, or at least a square of it. He climbed out FREEZING, because the water had turned to FLOATING ICE ISLANDS, and set the timer for two hundred more minutes and brushed his teeth until he was quite certain his gums were going to turn to hamburger and he would be toothless. Then he went into his bedroom, wore LAST NIGHT'S PAJAMAS, which no one had bothered to take to the laundry room and PROVIDE HIM WITH CLEAN ONES, and climbed into bed with the Boxcar Children book there wasn't a chance he'd get through two pages of. His mother didn't come and didn't come, and then he heard her laughing on the phone to her sister—it was always her sister who made her laugh that way.

He couldn't sleep and couldn't sleep and couldn't sleep so he snuck out of bed and into the living room, where he used a ruler from last school year to straighten the magazines on the coffee table, which were lying HITHER SKITHER AND YON. He tried to tackle the kitchen but very possibly only made things worse. There were Emergency Flashlights in every drawer and in the pantry and pretty much all over the place, so Kaline took one of those and went out to the yard. Two of the yellow yard signs were leaning sideways like the Tower of Peepers in Italy, which was Italian for France, so he straightened those. He walked down the driveway with a thump thump in his chest and opened the door to his dad's garage, leaving the light off so his mother wouldn't know he was out there. He shone the Emergency Flashlight on only one thing: the wall where his father's woodworking tools hung on hooks and pegs, each tool as clean as the day it was pur- chased, and h a n g i n g level in a way Kaline  would never master. His dad would NOT leave his tools forever. He would come back for them— their very straightness told Kaline so. The sight of them, perfect the way his dad was, the opposite of crooked like Kaline himself, made him have a sick feeling and also his throat started to ache, so he went back in the house and crept up the stairs to his bed, and somehow he drifted off to sleep with Banjo and in short everything was one hundred percent out of control.

By the end of the week, Skracky, Devil Tooth, and Mr. Zero had stolen virtually everything Kaline owned, including the things he had replaced with the things they'd stolen earlier. Every day he wore two pairs of school pants, but he couldn't wear two belts, so the *inside* pants slid down inside the *outside* ones and there was no way around it: the double-pants situation was making him bonkers. So far the men hadn't made good on their promise to remove of him his clothing, but they kept threatening. FURTHERMORE, as his dad would say, Kaline was about to know the defeat of homelessness, as no one was going to let him stay in the third grade without a single possession. Oh sure, in the evenings he'd get to go home, but during the day he would have to take to dwelling in tunnels and under bridges, like the billy goats.

On Friday night Kaline sat at the dinner table without tooting or speaking or moving. His spirit was thoroughly broken. He was going to have to tell his mother that they would need to go back to the Super Humongnous Department Store and replace every single school item, including the dry-erase markers and lightbulbs for the classroom.

His mother looked concerned, in place of where she usually looked exhausted. "You doing all right?" she asked, watching Kaline sit so listlessly.

"Yes, thank you." It was a lie, but he couldn't tell his mom, who seemed a bit on the BROKEN side herself, the truth. On and on his problems marched, the grass growing, the lining up of the table on the floor squares, the stolen school materials, his missing father, WHO BY THE WAY Kaline had now realized had either been kidnapped by the Mafia or turned into werewolf food and his mother didn't want to tell him and he didn't blame her. She was treating the situation in the way they handled the death of Great-Granddad Homer: say nothing and eventually Kaline will forget Great-Granddad ever existed. On the few occasions he did inquire, his mother had said breezily, "He's having a long nap in another place." IN ANOTHER PLACE was what she said, and the next day at school he asked Coach Joe if he perchance knew where that place was, because Great-Granddad Homer carried both chewing gun AND a harmonica, and Kaline wanted them during naptime. Coach Joe put a kindly hand on Kaline's shoulder and said, "No son, no I do not know."

"Well, is there anything you'd like to tell me about school this week?" his mother asked. Kaline was nearly shocked out of his school pants. His mom never DARED ask a question like that, for fear of the length of time Kaline was able to go on and on about his day, often telling the truth but periodically getting the day mixed up with an episode of *Power Rangers*. Hours could pass and he would still be talking. DAYS could pass, and they would have only gotten to the fourth of seventeen jaw-dropping adventures.

"Not much to tell." Kaline scooted his carrots around. The steamed carrot was his sworn enemy for life, and he had to somehow make his mother believe he'd eaten some or she'd torture him by sprinkling them with BROWN SUGAR as if this were an IMPROVEMENT.

His mother looked at him, looked back at the paper.

Kaline continued to sit very still.

"Hey!" she said, with a forced excitement. "There's a circus coming to town."

Kaline, in his nearly hypmotized state, barely heard her, but there came to life in his mind an entire universe: a man on stilts wearing pants with broad stripes. A lion in the cage that ROARED with anger! A dancing bear, and poodles jumping through flaming hoops, and a man in a top hat, and so many other details. He could smell the popcorn and cotton candy, and he could feel the sawdust under his feet, and also the hot smells of the animals—all of it so different from his square of life and house and yard on Hoppadoppalous Court. He could have stayed there forever.

"Did you SAW that?" Kaline shouted, meaning did his mother see the incredible dive the Girl on the Flying Trapeze had taken?

"Kaline?" His mother put her hand over his arm.

"What?" He looked around at his kitchen. The salt and pepper shakers were misaligned and so he moved them. "Did I say something out loud?"

"Why don't you try to eat something?" His mother moved his plate closer to him, and in the gesture he could feel the threat of the terrible brown sugar, and so he put a bit of carrot in his mouth and then with extreme sneakiness let the half-chewed bite fall down into his shirt. He would deal with that later.

They continued to sit in silence for a few more minutes, his mother periodically glancing up at him in concern, and then she said, reading another ad in the paper, "Oh, look at this interesting article. They've begun to build tree houses for whole families. Grown-up tree houses."

And JUST LIKE THAT Kaline Klattermaster's life changed. Because as he watched, a tree house went up in the woods and it was ENORMOUS—there were two floors at least, and ramps for motorcycles, and all the furniture was shaped like food. The hot-dog-shaped couch was really a gigantic piece of foam with pretend ketchup on it. He saw every room: there was ivy twisting through the window in the kitchen, which was filled with the ingredients for s'mores, and a little treelet was growing up through the dining room floor and dropping fruit on the table, only Kaline didn't know what kind of fruit it was. He had his own bedroom with a hole cut directly in the ceiling so he could watch the stars at night, and his bed was filled with helium, so he could float about the room SHOULD HE WISH TO. He wandered from room to room and then there was a mighty racket and up the motorcycle ramp drove a dark-haired guy on a HUGE motorcycle, and that guy stopped and said, "Hey Kaline! It's me, your brother, Steve!" And Kaline shook his hand, and it was so strong—it was CIRCUS MAN STRONG. There was a rumbling downstairs as a fast car parked, and then barreling up the stairs was another guy and along with him ONE HUNDRED PUPPIES. He too shook Kaline's hand and said,

"Hey,
dude! I'm Nicky,
your other brother,
and these are your puppies!" The puppies jumped
and danced all around him, licking his hands and
making little barks, and Kaline didn't know what

to say; somehow it had all come true, and he had gotten his wish.

"Kaline? Mr. Daydreamer? Do you want dessert?" his mother asked.

He looked down at his plate and felt the cold place where the half-chewed carrots were nesting in his shirt. "But I didn't eat my dinner."

"Oh who cares," his mom said, taking his plate away. "Those carrots were awful, anyway."

"Just to ask you: do you happen to know where Dad is?"

Kaline's mother ruffled his cowlick. "Not around here, that's for sure."

PART TWO

Chapter Five

THE TREE HOUSE

Praise the powers that be, Steve was GOOD AT
HISTORY! And Nicky was good at nearly everything else, although mostly he was a good mechanic.
Every evening Kaline took his homework and went
to the tree house, and they all sat together and
worked through things, and even though sometimes Steve didn't know the answer and Kaline
tried to guess it on his own, mostly they did okay.

After homework they ate s'mores and then took
the motorcycle out for a spin with the puppies in a
special sidecar. The puppies all wore little helmets,

with flaps that streamed beside them in the wind, along with their tongues. It was MAYHEM IN DOGVILLE! Nicky followed in his fast car, and some-times he wanted to race, and then they would all FLY down the dark roads around Hoppadoppalous Court, and Steve would say, "Watch what happens when I turn my headlights off," and behind them Nicky would do the same, and they would all be cast into the most serious darkness, and because he couldn't see where the road ended and the motor-cycle began, Kaline felt like he was soaring above the ground, free of gravity.

They rescued a baby bear stuck in a tree, and WHO KNEW THERE WERE BEARS ON KALINE'S STREET, and they stopped for Slurpees at a drive-in where all the waitresses were on roller skates. Sometimes Kaline brought Banjo along, and he could tell the dog was having a WHALE of a time with them. He'd spent his whole life without any friend but Kaline and then suddenly there were ONE HUNDRED. Banjo had been asking if he could visit Maestro, but was that a good idea? Was Maestro a dog person? Would he play . . . too *rrruffff*, as Scooby would say? And what did Kaline know, STILL ANYWAY, about Mr. P.?

"Hey," Kaline said, as they all drank their Slurpees. "What do you know of this man Mr. Osiris Putnaminski?"

Steve set his drink down on his tray. "Mr. P.? He's great. Great fella. He helped me get my first bike, not this one but the purple one before it. He knew right where to find it. He a friend of yours?"

"No," Kaline said, shaking his head. "He's still a stranger."

"Stranger?!?" Steve said. "He's a little strange, but he's no stranger. Have you seen what's in his basement?"

Kaline thought about it. That's what he had often heard talked about: Mr. P.'s basement, his hobby. But he assumed it was something boring. "No—what's down there?"

"Nope, no can do, Mr. Klattermaster. You've got to see it for yourself."

At dinner Kaline REGALED (which meant he said A LOT OF THINGS) (another word for REGALED, according to his dad, was TOR-TURED) his mother with tales of his adventures with his brothers in the tree house, and all the things they'd done over the past few days. He told her EVERYTHING, and when he began describing each of the puppies individually, including its name and the color of its collar, his mother held her hand up like a traffic cop and said STOP.

"For one thing," she began, "you have gradually scooted your chair back against the cabinets. Bring it back to the table."

Kaline did so.

"For another, you have slowly acquired a little mountain of butternut squash inside your T-shirt, and it's beginning to leak through."

Kaline looked down. "Ruh-roh."

"And finally"—his mom smiled at him, something she hadn't done for quite a while—"do you tell the people at school about the tree house? About Steve and Nicky and the puppies?"

Kaline paused a moment. He didn't know exactly how to explain his position on that one. He had a very strong sense that the people at school wouldn't understand. Like if he had mentioned to THEM there was a circus in town, they would have heard the word and MAYBE gotten a little picture in their heads, but otherwise the whole thing would have just floated by like smoke or a balloon, circus gone. And if he told anyone about the tree house, they might see it but they wouldn't really SEE it, and because of that they could never really visit, and so what was the use? Plus the Skracky gang would make fun and do unto Kaline physical hurts he didn't want to consider. "No," he told her. "I don't tell anyone at school about it."

She gave him another smile—this one only halfway. "Okay then. That's fine. Tell me more about the puppy named Apex."

In thanks for them helping him with his home-work, Kaline decided to help Steve and Nicky with their own business, which was comic books. They were thinking of making an animated film but that was somewhere in the future, when they were all better at drawing and knew their story more completely.

The comic strip they'd been working on for some time was called *Stumpy*, and it was about a stump in a forest and the creatures that came to visit him every day. They chose Stumpy because he was one of the few things Kaline could help draw. Crazy things happened to Stumpy! Two squirrels got in a fight on top of him once, and they became so mad they spun around in a circle, one squirrel chasing the other's tail, until they were just a blur! Stumpy became snow-covered; a fat man sat down on him and FARTED; termites began amassing at the borders and threatened to descend, until the army ants gathered and fought them off.

Their next strip was called *Sandwichy*, because Kaline could CERTAINLY draw a sandwich, and then Nicky had the great idea to call him Sandwich On A Stick because then he could hop around and wouldn't have to wait for people to come to him! Oh the adventures Sandwich On A Stick had! He had to out-hop the terrible evil remote-controlled car of a boy who looked exactly like Skracky, whose comic-book name was "Skracky." A character named "Devil Tooth" kept trying to take a bite out of him with his hideous pointy-out eyetooth! And a boy named "Mr. Nothing" (Kaline was proud of this change) tried to break off Sandwich On A Stick's stick, thereby rendering him once again merely a sandwich, to which things happened.

"Whew!" Kaline said, after they'd filled another notebook with adventures. "I'm pretty sure we're ready to start on that movie soon. You guys are going to have to go to the Big Persons' library and get some books on what we do next."

Steve and Nicky shook their heads, thoughtful. "Yeah," Steve agreed, "we should get on that. But have I told you my idea for a series about a villain called Fat Raccoon, who uses his little black paws to get into windows and steal all the candy in the house?"

Kaline smacked himself in the head. "That's BRILLIANT. Okay, ixnay on the oviemay. We obviously have more books to write."

They drew for a while, and then Nicky got up to get them all hot chocolate.

"Hey," Kaline asked, trying to sound casual, "just asking, have any of you seen my dad?"

Steve glanced at Nicky, but then looked back down at his comic strip. "Nope, boss. 'Fraid not."

"Yeah, well." Kaline picked up a black marker to trace his new sandwich. "That man is like the wind."

Chapter Six

BULLIES!

At school the following Monday, Skracky, Devil Tooth, and Mr. Zero stood before Kaline's desk while MRS. WHY DOES SHE EVEN BOTHER GOTTLIEB was gone some place or other.

"Hey," Skracky said, smacking the top of Kaline's head and making his cowlick go boinga-boinga. "D'joo bring me that Yu-Gi-Oh! deck like I told you, along with the super-rare Japanese Blue Eyes White Dragon card?"

"And"—Devil Tooth leaned close, nearly poking out Kaline's eye with his protuberance—"did you bring me those Ninja headbands I wanted?"

"AND," added Mr. Zero, "you might as well just give me your lunchbox right now, I'm hungry."

Kaline sighed.

Skracky smiled and it was like the smile of a MAN-EATING SHARK. "Time for the pants, too, Cowlick."

Every evening he'd taken money out of his of special savings box and gone to the corner store and bought these goons what they demanded, but now he was in trouble.

"You've been doing WHAT?" Steve had asked when Kaline told him about the situation. They were FLABBERGASTED and APPALLED. Steve declared himself GOBSTOPPED.

"Well!" Kaline threw his arms up in flustergastion. "What am I supposed to do? You should see the size of these men! Taken together they are roughly as big as the mall." While it was the case that Kaline was far more comfortable in just the one pair of trousers, they were the last he owned, and if . . . he couldn't think about it. If, tomorrow? He could NOT think about it. If they decided to de-pants him again he would be—NO. NOT THINKING ABOUT IT.

Steve sat down on one side of Kaline, Nicky on the other. "It doesn't matter what size they are; they'll just fall harder. Look, Kaline. Everyone has to suffer bullies—why, there are bullies everywhere! They're at your school and at the gas station, and some kids have parents who are bullies so they NEVER get away from them. They're in our government, and once in a while you hear that an actor in a movie is a bully and no one wants to work with him! You have to learn to deal with this. You can't just empty out that box and hope their meanness will someday end, because it won't."

"I understand all that," Kaline said, tugging at the neckline of his T-shirt. "But I don't know HOW to deal with them without risking my ears and my last pair of pants."

Steve and Nicky both thought about it. The puppies sat down quietly and thought about it.

"Beat them up," Nicky said, with enthusiasm. "Hide behind something and when they come around a corner, BLAMMO! Hit them with a piece of lumber."

Steve nearly jumped off the muffin-shaped chair. "NO NO! Kaline, no. You must not try to fight with them. That only works with bullies on television and in comic strips. No—you have to use what you have, your own strength."

"What I HAVE?" Kaline asked, raising both eyebrows. "Should I tie them up with my size 16 uniform sleeves? Tell them a bunch of jokes I learned from my Scooby-Doo book? Tell *my dad*?"

"Okay," Steve had said, nodding. "True enough. But you've got us. And I remember a time in my own life when I was in some trouble like this, and you know who helped me?"

"The Green Hornet?"

"Mr. Osiris Putnaminski. None other."

Kaline thanked them—thanked his brothers—and helped get the puppies tucked in for the night. Then he went back into his own house where he found his mother knitting and watching television. She had started an afghan some time before his dad vanished, POOF, gone, and she'd been working on it in a way Kaline didn't want to tell her was a bit *loony tunes*. Maybe she would notice on her own, given that she was now using whatever yarn she could find, so the thing *looked* crazy, and also she didn't seem to realize that blankets *stop* at some point.

He sat down beside her on the couch. "Hey," he said, covering up the tops of his legs with one end of the thing being spun, inch by inch, out of her knitting needles. "Is this afghan for the house?"

"We can keep it if you want to, or we can give it to someone as a gift."

"No, I mean do you intend to stand on the roof and COVER THE ENTIRE HOUSE WITH IT?"

Kaline's mother stopped knitting. Her eyes wandered over the acres of yarn madness spread out before her. "Wow."

"You see."

"I do. I think I'll keep at it, though. I like it the way it is."

"Fine with me." They sat that way for a little while. Kaline tried to swing his legs, but more of the afghan had slipped over him and he might as

well have been trapped under a school bus. "Just
to ask you, is Mr. Putnaminski our friend?"

His mom looked at him over the top of her
glasses. She had to scoot them down to the end of
her nose for knitting. "Mr. P.? Of course he is! I've
known him my whole life, and so have you. He's
been our neighbor since before you were born!
He used to hold you when you were a baby, and
sometimes push your stroller on walks. You *loved*
Mr. P. when you were a baby."

"But I don't know him anyway, without regards
of things you just said. Now tell me why that is,
if he and I were *moocha comp-**ah**-droze* when I
was a tot."

Kaline's mother stared at him. "What language
is that you're using?"

"It is the language called Spanish, *el Spanyo*. I
am entirely like a fluid in speaking it."

She went back to knitting. "Your father . . .

worried about you, he kept a close eye on you. And you were a happy baby, but shy, and you got more and *more* shy and comfortable only with me or your dad. And you started hiding from everyone!"

Kaline could almost remember. He could just barely remember standing behind his dad's legs at the grocery store, hiding from someone who had come up to say hello, slipping behind his dad to make himself invisible, HE HOPED.

"Ever since you were three, four? If Osiris walked down the sidewalk with his cane and his dog—it used to be a much bigger dog, a bull mastiff—you would run around and spin and fall down on the ground like a Tasmanian devil, and then you'd hide. He probably thinks you're insane."

"I'm not insane!"

"I'm just saying."

"Well."

"You march to the beat of your own drummer, let's say." Kaline's mom put down her knitting needles and patted the top of Kaline's head.

Ruh-roh, Kaline thought.

That evening Kaline twirled around and around on the porch until he got dizzy and fell down. It turned out the porch was secretly made of some gluey stuff, so he got stuck and had to try to peel himself up one piece at a time. He sang "Casper the Friendly Ghost," then realized that Casper was a little dead boy WAS HE NOT? So Kaline lay back down and tried to imagine being dead but WHEW that didn't work.

Then he heard it, the opening and closing of Mr. P.'s door, which meant the evening's Declamation of Inkdependence, and Kaline jumped up as if he had not a lick of shyness in him. He walked down the sidewalk and stood at the place his walkway ended. Mr. P. strolled toward him, and Maestro's little paws ticka ticka ticka-ed on the sidewalk.

"Why, good evening, Mr. Klattermaster."

"Good evening, okay." An insane thing to say.

"Mr. Klattermaster, please meet Maestro properly. Maestro, sit."

The little white dog plopped his bottom down on the ground, and when Kaline bent toward him the dog rose up and held one paw out for Kaline to shake. In a fit of lunacy, Kaline took the paw and at the same time curtsied and said, "Pleased to meet you for real."

WHAT?!? HE CURTSIED?!? Maestro wasn't the King of Siam and Kaline wasn't a girl!

"Very nice," Mr. P. said. "Excellent

style. Would you like to walk with us?"

Kaline glanced back at the house but he knew his mom wouldn't mind. He shrugged, but started walking.

"What would you like to talk about today, I wonder? How school is wastesing all your free time and et cetera?"

The answer required special thought, so Kaline jumped like a frog over one square of sidewalk, a second, hopped on one foot, tooted his imaginary bugle for luck. "See there are these bullies at my school, maybe you are thinking of bullies you knew back when people had only worms to eat but these are A VERY DIFFERENT SORT. They are . . . I believe they might be grown-ups in school clothes and they have robbed me of everything and every piece of money I own, my money box is 100 PERCENT EMPTY, they steal my pants, they smell, one of them has a single eyebrow which gives me bad dreams. NOW. I asked . . . *a friend of mine* what I should do, no, two friends, and one said to strike them with lumber, but the other said no hitting, AS IF I COULD HIT ALL THREE, it would be like bowling a strike at the Bowl-A-Rama. IMPOSSIBLE. So this ONE friend of mine said you, Mr. Putnaminski, might have some advice which is why I am here. On the sidewalk axing you—asking you—ummm, see? What? Do I do?"

Mr. P. stopped walking. Maestro sat down. The man seemed to be thinking very hard about the situation. He thought and thought and then said, "Bullies are certainly the bane of youth. Do you know the meaning of that word 'bane'?"

"Yes," Kaline said, "I believe it is an action fig-ger with a karate-chop arm."

"Perhaps. But it also means the *curse* of elementary school, the *worst* part. Now when

I was eating worms we had a variety of ways of dealing with bullies, most of them not good. What I've learned about bullies is that they are often stupid—forgive my unkindness—and they are often afraid. So sometimes it helps to use quite big words to confuse them. Make the words up if you have to."

"I myself am not very bright. One of the bullies calls me Dumb As A Box of Dead Frogs. That would be Devil Tooth, who calls me that."

"I think you're much smarter than you give yourself credit for. But honestly, Mr. Klatter-master? If I were you I'd do the smartest thing of all: *I'd tell my mother*."

They had come back around the block and were in front of Kaline's house. He automatically went over to straighten the grass signs, which were now nearly invisible because the grass itself was so tall.

"That's nice of you, to keep your dad's things up like that. He's a fine man. A bit *tight*."

"What does that mean?" Kaline asked, staring at Mr. P.

"Oh, you know, do you ever put on a shirt and you walk around in it an hour or so and then realize, 'This shirt is just too tight and it's making me uncomfortable'? Like that."

Hmmmmm. Mr. Putnaminski could be a decent fellow but clearly he was not right in the noggin because that last thing made NOT ONE PIECE OF SENSE.

Kaline skipped up his steps. "Bye, Mr. P.! Bye, Maestro!" He was inside before he realized he'd meant to say thank you but it just never came out.

"You're telling me," Kaline's mother said, leaning over her coffee cup after hearing his story, "that these boys have stolen everything from you, and all your saved money, and even your PANTS?"

"Yes, ma'am."

"You weren't making it up?"

Kaline stared at her. Could she not SEE that he was missing his clothing, that he owned no school supplies, that he had barely saved his ear holes from destruction and now the ear flaps pointed in pretty much TWO DIFFERENT DIRECTIONS?

"Well. No. Why would I?"

His mother sat back in her chair. She looked off into the distance and didn't say another word.

Chapter Seven

THE RULES OF THE TREE HOUSE!

Nutrition is very important, therefore:

1. S'mores must be consumed every day, as a single s'more has all the vitamins a child needs, plus, as Nicky said, they make our fur shiny.
2. Oranges are a very good fruit. Why? Because they are round like a BALL and can be used in place of a softball (lost it), a baseball (dogs ate it, pooped it back out all over the yard), a tennis ball (peeled it apart

in a science experiment that did not involve school, or science). Which leads us to . . .

3. ORANGE DRINK! ORANGE DRINK! What does it mean? Nobody knows! What is in it? Nobody cares!

4. All Things Gummi. When Kaline mentions the words, Steve and Nicky and all the puppies stop and look deadly serious. They do not distinguish between the Gummi Octopus, the Gummi Worm, the Gummi Rat, the Gummi Alligator, nor even the lowly Gummi Bear. Because all are equally holy, and indeed, are the one thing that can make anyone feel loved and full of hope.

5. Strawberry Fluff. No further comment required.

6. Slim Jims. Slim Jims are made of buffalo meat, TANG, and the secret stuff taken

into space by the Russians, something involving monkeys and teeny-tiny batteries, all of it wrapped in casing. The casing is meant to be eaten, as a test of courage, and is actually quite delicious.

"Whew!" Nicky said. He could eat more than anyone Kaline had ever met. The tree house looked as if a giant had picked it up and shaken it and now they were in Upside-Down Land. Indeed, the hot-dog sofa *was* upside down, some things that had been on the floor were now stuck to the ceiling, and Slim Jim wrappers were floating around in the breeze like long skinny butterflies missing their wings. Fifteen jars of Strawberry Fluff were empty, spoons stuck inside them (spoons stuck inside them permanently, sadly). Some of the puppies were being unusually quiet, and Kaline realized it was because their mouths were glued shut with Gummis. *Hmmm*, he thought, *this is important to know*. The s'mores machine had worked so hard and produced so many gluey sandwiches that it had begun to smoke, and before anyone could panic Kaline said, "Allow me." He pulled the fire extinguisher (of COURSE he'd thought to put one up here) off the wall, and standing PRECISEDLY like Fireman Flip—legs about a foot apart, a look of hard, angry manliness on his face—Kaline had pulled the pin, flipping it over his shoulder where it hit one puppy on the snoot. The puppy was unable to bark or yip because his mouth was in Gummi Jail. Kaline pointed the white hose at the s'mores machine and then gave it his all, he opened it FULL THROTTLE, as Steve liked to say.

Kaline felt the extinguisher pause in his hand, rearing back like a stallion. RUH-ROH, it was maybe a little bit possible that he'd put one of the INDUSTRIAL-SIZE FFFAWL-approved devices in the tree house, because the white fluff of heroism came out the end of the hose with such INSANE FORCE that the s'mores maker was blown off the table, through a window, and waaaaay out into the open air, where it hovered a moment and then fell down down down with a chocolatey/marshmallowy crash. Kaline himself was thrown about fifteen feet or 100 yards across the living room, landing on a banana chair. The hose was going WILD! spraying foam all over everything—the ceiling, the furniture, the puppies, the brothers. Kaline slipped off the banana chair and the hose dragged him all around the house, up the stairs where he bonk bonk bonked his head, and down the stairs, where he bonk bonk bonked his head, and all the while Kaline was yelling, "Help! Help! It's got me, the evil thing has me and I can't let go!"

Steve yelled, "Just let go!"

Nicky yelled, "Let go of it, Kaline!"

Kaline shouted back, "I can't let go! It has my hands stuck upon itself as if by nuclear magnets! This is doom, DOOM I SAY!!!"

The worst of the momentum was over, and Kaline was slithering about in the foam like a beached albino seal. He tried to stand up, slipped, went right back down. Around him Steve and Nicky were

trying to get to him. They too slipped and fell, tried to stand. The dogs were all rolling around, leaping through extinguisher drifts. One little guy seemed to be trapped somewhere, yipping and scared. The boys dug through the mountains and hills and there was Banjo, completely covered with extinguishment!

"Banjo!"

"Banjo!"

"Poor little fella!"

The other dogs surrounded him. They tugged at his collar, dragged a clean towel over his head, licked him. Within minutes they were playing like a pack of hyenas, and Banjo was having so much fun Kaline could only watch him and laugh, and Steve and Nicky laughed.

Steve said, "Man, this place is a *mess*."

Nicky shook his head. "It's a slice of Disaster Pie."

Kaline said, "Want me to go get another fire extinguisher? There are about twenty in the garage."

Steve stared at Kaline a moment. "HECK YEAH WE DO!"

Kaline said, "One for each of us!"

So they started all over.

Chapter Eight

THE HERO

At school the next day the beasts approached his desk while his teacher, whose name he could barely remember, had gone to the supply closet for something. Kaline rose to his full height, which was very short. He tried to gesture toward the goons without actually hitting one of them with his sleeves. He remembered Mr. P. saying that often bullies were stupid—forgive the unkindness— and to make up big words if necessary. So he said, "It's over, you pus-filled gigantoids. I'm not giving you any more presents or letting you steal

KALINE KLATTERMASTER'S TREE HOUSE

anything else from me. I've been nice about it so far because I have felt sorry for you, as you are clearly brain-damaged and have no future outside of our federal penitentiary system, which is jail in case you were wondering."

Skracky seemed to get LARGER, and his eyes got SMALLER, making him look like a very angry wild pig about to stick a tusk in a beagle dog. "You said WHAT?"

Kaline remained calm. By now, many of his classmates were paying attention, especially those who had been buying the *other* decks of trading cards and the *other* basketball paraphernalia demanded by the three. "I said that I am finished feeling sorry for you and providing for you. If you want more Yu-Gi-Oh! cards I suggest you get a job, perhaps on a pirate's ship, or maybe as one of those men who picks up large dead farm animals for the county."

Devil Tooth was actually pulling back a fist like in an old Western; he was ACTUALLY going to SOCK Kaline in the KISSER.

"Whoa now," Skracky said, pulling D. T.'s arm back. "Let's give Cowlick a chance to dig himself in even farther. You're done, you say."

"I am done." Kaline made a gesture with his hands: finished. "If you continue to harass me I will be forced to turn you over to my older brothers Steve and Nicky, who, if they DON'T scalp you and leave you running around like babies, will turn you over to their ONE HUNDRED DOGS, and if that doesn't work, Nicky will run you down with his race car."

All three boys stood motionless. They made attempts at puzzlement, but mostly their faces stayed the same.

"You've got brothers?" Mr. Zero finally asked.

"Indeed. I have two. And they've been very patient with you, but their patience has run out, and so has mine."

"One of 'em's got a race car?" D. T. asked, sneering, revealing even more of the dreaded dental apparatus.

"Yes," Kaline said, his voice filled with confidence. "He has a Santiago Zeppelin, circa 1989, one of only six made in the world. It's a V-14 and can pull either sixteen horses or twenty-four sled dogs. He has added a shammy that runs on rocket fuel, and tires that inflate to the size of a small shed, in order to traverse rivers and streams. It has an original Opus 14 in D-Flat engine, many things on the floor, and glass pipes that can't be broken even with a sledgehammer. It's a car you would NOT want as your ENEMY. And don't get me started on Steve's motorcycle."

The three stood in front of Kaline's desk, confused. "Why do we never see them?" Skracky asked. "Why don't they pick you up at school?"

"Because," Kaline said, affecting a noble warrior stance, "they have jobs, and I was trying to protect you from them. But if it's time for me to call them in, I will."

The whole room sat silent. The little ragtag goon army considered its options, then gave Kaline one final little shove and walked away. As they passed Georgia's desk they knocked all her books and papers to the ground, in search of their next victim. They had stopped at the desk of a boy who looked about to cry when the classroom door flew open and Kaline's mother came sailing in as if pushed by a mighty wind. The principal was behind her, looking squinched in the face.

"YOU!" Kaline's mother said in a voice like thunder, pointing to the Skrackys. The rhinestones and sequins on her glasses flashed as if she had lightning in them! "Get out into this hallway RIGHT NOW. Your parents are on their way here, the POLICE are on their way, and you'd better hope they all arrive before I get my hands on you."

For a long time, maybe six hours, no one in the class spoke. Then Georgia leaned over to Kaline's desk and said, "I have a big brother too. He works for the county, picking up dead farm animals."

Kaline's eyes widened. "SERIOUSLY? HOW COOL IS THAT?"

It took him all day with the dreaded pencil and the wide-ruled paper, but by the last bell Kaline had written out what he wanted to say to Skracky. He dropped the note on the boy's desk as he went to his locker. It said:

ANd AlsO LEavE GEorjiA AlonE to Her bRotHer Has a PITCH FORK

Chapter Nine

THE TRUTH!

"You have worn me plumb OUT!" Kaline shouted, after playing basketball with Steve and Nicky for what seemed sixteen hours. They were playing on the backyard grass, even though it was really tall. Steve and Nicky turned out to be VERY good basketball players, and had even been able to fashion a hoop where Kaline didn't have one, and then to get a basketball when the only ball Kaline had was from the grocery store and had a bright picture of Cowboy Woody on the side.

"You boys need to give me a REST!" Kaline

said, bending over to catch his breath. At the same time his mom opened the back door and called him in.

"I'll be there in a minute!" Kaline shouted back. "I need to make sure my muscles don't freeze!"

"Now, Kaline."

In the kitchen his mom had already made him a glass of chocolate milk, and there was a fresh cup of coffee at her place at the table. She asked him to sit down.

A strange fear filled Kaline's body. He knew, suddenly, that she was going to tell him what had happened to his father. He mentally went through the list of possibilities, counting on his fingers as he went:

1. Abducted by extra-terrestriums. If returned, will be a pod.
2. Captured by those kinds of spies who are

after James Bond. Some are women who like to kiss. Kaline shuddered.

3. Was hit by a falling piano while making a silent film.

4. WHAAAT? That didn't make sense even to Kaline.

5. Had become the Undead.

6. Gnawed upon by jackals.

7. Was wandering the desert with amnesia. Covered with scorpion bites and seeing water where there was none.

"Your father," his mother began, looking down at her coffee cup, "has rented a condominium on the other side of town. He wanted to have some Alone Time, and he has been enjoying it so much he's decided to get a divorce. You and I are going to drive into town today to visit an attorney, so we can help your dad get what he's looking for."

Kaline didn't move.

"Do you understand what I'm saying, sweetheart? He and I aren't going to be married anymore."

Everything in the room became blurry. Kaline tried to take a breath but he couldn't—it seemed he couldn't breathe. But even though he was shortly going to suffocate, his heart went on beating: he could hear it pounding. "This is because of me, isn't it?" Kaline asked finally, his hand shaking as he put his chocolate milk glass down. "Because of dinnertime and 'you are making us physically ill with dizziness' and all that."

"No!" his mother said, leaning toward him so quickly Kaline backed up and nearly tipped his chair over. "No, it has nothing to do with you. Your father loves you more than anything in the world."

"If that was true, he wouldn't leave," Kaline said, crossing his arms. He was horribly afraid he might cry. A DIVORCE was so much better than what he'd feared and so much worse than what he'd thought possible he could barely get his mind to work at all. If it had been aliens or werewolves or a Bond villain at least there would have been the POSSIBILITY of Kaline rescuing him. But this? This was something Kaline had absolutely no control over.

"Kaline, it's *me*. It's me he doesn't want to live with. I think he'd be happy living here with you for the rest of his life. He could have the same schedule every day, and he could adjust it as you got older. You'd have meatloaf on Mondays, chicken on Tuesdays, you'd do your grocery shopping at the same time every Wednesday evening. You'd watch the same programs on television at the same time, and set the timer for every activity, and each vacation would be planned out to the MINUTE, and there would be no stopping until it was on the PLAN SHEET. He *loves* taking care of you—you are the *meaning* in his life. That's why he's stayed away and thought about it so hard, because it was a very difficult decision for him to reach, and not the way he wanted things to go."

"I think I'm going to throw up," Kaline said, feeling pale.

"Go to the bathroom, then," his mother said.

"I'm not going to throw up, I just thought it for a second."

The two sat silently. Kaline's milk grew warm and his mother's coffee got too cold to drink, and then she told him to go get changed because they needed to drive into town.

Kaline took a few moments to lay down on his bed with Banjo. He closed his eyes and visited the tree house, where Steve and Nicky and all the puppies were sitting around very sadly. The puppies weren't even licking anything. The motorcycle wasn't running, the car was just sitting under the tree. So they knew then. Maybe they had known all along. He would go tell them everything when he got back.

His mother drove down the straight streets of Hoppadoppalous Court, driving past houses that all looked the same, and then turned left and drove down a street where all the houses looked the same, and turned right, and turned left, and Kaline couldn't even tell where they were because everything was identical to everything else. At night he often fell asleep in the tree house, but when he wakened in the morning he was in his bed. It was a mystery. Sometimes he walked to the edge of the backyard and stood against the chain-link fence and wondered how to go farther; for just a moment he couldn't remember how to GET THERE, to the tree house. Kaline leaned over and bonked his head against the window.

When they reached the edge of the subdivision they stopped at a stop sign and across the street was a large stand of trees, 4 or 5 or perhaps 700 acres of woods. Kaline's heart pounded in his chest, and he grabbed his mother's arm. "Is that it?!?" he yelled, pointing to the woods. "Is that where the tree house is?"

She glanced at him a moment and looked sad, but then she had plenty to be sad about. She patted his arm, pulled him close to her, and kissed the top of his head. "I don't know, sweetheart. I don't know where it is."

That night Steve and Nicky made him a special dinner of s'mores and real hot dogs, not couches, and then they sat at the table and talked. They all agreed it was a bummer, and then Steve went through Kaline's list of worries and set everything in order. HE, Steve, would ask a friend he knew to cut the lawn, he declared, and he would simply remove the yellow signs because grass was meant to be walked on. And since it was only his dad who worried about the alignments of square and rectangular objects, there was no reason not to let them get all catty-whompus, if his mom didn't mind and OBVIOUSLY she did not. If Kaline wanted to keep using the egg timer, then Nicky would show him for certain what was twenty minutes, and on the whole they made him feel much better.

"Here's all I can say, small buddy," Steve said, patting Kaline on the back. "Be kind to everyone you can be, and be patient. Everyone is doing the best they can. And remember that not one single day has ever been like the day before it, so there's not a chance in this world tomorrow is going to look like today."

Kaline thanked them—thanked his brothers— and helped get the puppies tucked in for the night. Then he went back into his own house where he found his mother knitting and watching television. He sat down beside her on the couch. "Hey," he said, covering up the tops of his legs with her afghan. "You're wearing your craziest hat." It was made of green and blue squares and filled with holes, which what sense did that make anyway.

"Hey yourself," she said, pulling him close to her. "My ears were cold."

"You, ummm, you were pretty much like a superhero at my school except without any, you know, powers."

"Thank you. Put your feet up, take a load off."

Kaline put his feet up on the coffee table next to his mother's. The magazines scattered and a couple fell on the floor and it seemed like neither one of them, Kaline or his mom, cared.

Chapter Ten

THE BASEMENT

Saturday morning was the day. He had received a formal, handwritten invitation. Kaline was going next door, into the HAUNTED HEAP OF BRICK DWELLING, GIGANTIC SANTA WHO HAD A "HOBBY" in the BASEMENT. Mr. P. had promised "refreshments," which Kaline hadn't had since a disastrous attempt at Cub Scouts, where he had been asked to leave for locating an ACTUAL bugle and blowing it for two straight hours.

He walked across the front yard, which had been mowed by a person called Christopher just as Steve had said, and was missing all the little yellow signs, just like Steve had promised, and across the driveway and into Mr. P.'s yard, where he was waiting.

"This is some kind of house," Kaline said. "Are the bricks all tumbling down, as Mrs. Jalopoly says?"

"Some, surely." Mr. P. looked around, made a sweeping gesture. "Six HUNDRED forty acres, my boy, that is what my father owned. One square mile. We grew corn and soybeans—there was a wheat field over there to the west. It was a fine way to grow up."

"Were there warriors swinging tree to tree then?"

"No, the Indians were long gone. I have a book that has all those dates in it, everything that has happened on this land. Would you like to see it sometime?"

What Kaline would really like to do is STEAL it and REMEMORIZE it and then POSSIBLY he would be visiting the fourth grade next year.

"He sold a lot of the land during the Depression, and then my mom sold even more when she and I couldn't farm alone. I was his only son, and my sister left the state to become a nun."

A NUN? THERE WAS SUCH A THING AS REAL NUNS?

"When the developers came in and bought out everyone else, all of our neighbors and even everyone we'd sold our own land to, I decided to stay put. I kept just these ten acres—they're all that's left of the original six hundred forty." By now they were standing in front of the brick monstrosity.

The house had a screened porch on the bottom, and its floor was covered with very small blue and yellow and pale green tiles. The front door was

HUGE and the wood seemed to be about SIX FEET THICK, and in the top of the door was a stained-glass flower that if Kaline were guessing was either an iris or a bundt cake.

Kaline could hear Maestro dancing around on the other side of the door, but he didn't bark. Mr. P. opened the door and they stepped inside, and Kaline was looking at a wonderland. The furniture was old and MASSIVELY LARGE but it also looked like a hobbit lived here. How could that be? Some of the doorways were just small arches, and there seemed to be hidden passages, but when Kaline looked right at them they disappeared.

Mr. P. had a fireplace so large Kaline could stand in it. (There was no fire. If there had been: RUH-ROH!) He had a collection of glassware brought over on the *Mayflower*, and miniature books, and in a wooden case, an especially DISGUSTING-LOOKING thing he said had been the horn that grew out of the head of a young girl. Kaline backed up, nearly stepping on Maestro's paws.

One of Mr. P.'s bathrooms was designed to look like a bathroom at a "tube station," as he called it, or one of the restrooms in the underground subway in London, during World War II. As far as Kaline could tell, that's EXACTLY what this bathroom looked like, although he had never seen the original and was still trying to come to grips with the phrase "tube station."

The kitchen was the BIGGEST KITCHEN Kaline had ever seen, and it looked EXACTLY LIKE A FARMHOUSE KITCHEN ON WALTON'S MOUNTAIN, *The Waltons* just happened to be one of Kaline's favorite television programs to watch in reruns with his mom. There was a big stove that burned LOGS, and an ICEBOX, and a table big enough for TWELVE OR SIXTY

PEOPLE. In the corner of the room Kaline spotted what he knew to be an old-fashioned ice cream maker. He knew because Great-Granddad Homer used to bring one to the Fourth of July party, along with his harmonica, back before he decided to take a long nap elsewhere. On the kitchen table were pumpkin cookies and apple cider, all waiting for Kaline.

"The upstairs is more of the same, and the attic—well, the attic is very interesting," Mr. P. said, "but perhaps you'd like to see the basement?"

And there it was: the moment of truth. In scary books and movies someone evil was FOREVER trying to lure a child into the basement, and if Kaline hadn't known better he would have turned himself back into a Tasmanian devil and gotten himself home. But it was also true that strange people aren't always strangers, and sometimes your neighbor is just your neighbor, and the basement is GOOD, not EVIL. "Okay," Kaline said.

They walked down the brightly lit stairs, which were painted red, and at the bottom Mr. P. flipped on a bank of lights, the kind you raise slowly on handles. For a moment, Kaline couldn't move at all, because what he was looking at was his entire town, from end to end, in miniature.

There was Main Street, and it looked EXACTLY like Main Street only not exactly, because everything seemed to be from some other time. There was the downtown library, and the lion outside that was missing an ear from a particularly bad winter. There were the individual lampposts, mailboxes, trash cans, and benches for sitting. And there were people everywhere—children walking down the street with their mothers, little boys pulling carts or walking dogs on pieces of rope.

"Where . . ." Kaline tried to ask where it had all come from.

"I make them myself," Mr. P. explained. "I carve them from balsa wood and then paint them. Now watch this." He threw another switch and the railroad went into operation. The steam car started up right in front of the grain elevator, and it *actually blew steam*, and from a distance a man called "All Aboard!" and the train began moving around the track, which surrounded the whole town.

"Kaline, look here," Mr. P. said, pointing to a house in the outlying farmland. "Recognize that?"

"It's your own house! It's the house we're standing in!"

"That's right. And here is our barn, and the silos, and the tractors. Here are our cattle, and some chickens. This is my mom—she's carrying grain out to feed the goats."

Kaline walked from one end of town to the other. He studied the barber shop; the gondola in the park, where two people were dancing in a twirl; the blinking light on an old hotel downtown. He studied all the farms, gone now and replaced by their square houses, and he listened to the train go round and round, blowing its whistle and sending up steam.

He'd seen other miniatures before—there was

a big one at the children's museum—but those were different. He couldn't figure out why. Maybe it was because in those, one part of town was in winter, so there could be Christmas trees, and in another place it was autumn, or spring. But that wasn't the case here.

"Mr. P." Kaline tried to figure out how to ask what he was thinking. "Is it . . . always the same day here?"

Mr. Putnaminski clapped his hands together in surprise and happiness. "Why, yes it is! And how clever of you to notice! See the date on the bank window, and the time on the clock? Those things never change. It is always September 19, 1945. Always that day."

Kaline studied the beautiful long cars, the men working in their fields with mule-drawn plows. "Why? Why is it always the same day?"

Mr. P. took a deep breath. "Because the war—

World War II, Kaline—ended on September 2 of that year, and by the nineteenth everyone had begun to wait for their husbands and fathers to come home. That's me," he said, pointing to a little boy standing on the platform of the train station. He blended in with all the other people standing there, women clutching their purses in front of them, old men tipping their hats. Just a little boy in a crowd.

Kaline swallowed, felt his chin quiver, the feeling he HATED MOST IN THE WORLD. "And did he? Did he come home?"

Mr. Putnaminski rested his hand on Kaline's shoulder, smiled tenderly. "No. No, he didn't. Sometimes," he said, straightening his beard, "I am tempted—now I say I am TEMPTED—to make a figure of him just stepping down out of that car. I could do it; I've got pictures of him from late in the war. He would just be stepping down from this step right here—I would only barely be able to see him because of this slightly plump woman in front of me—but I would see him. I've been tempted to feel that, just for a moment."

"But you never."

Mr. P. shook his head. "No. It is better to be honest."

Kaline got to hold Maestro's leash as they walked down the street, and Mr. P. asked him question after question. Kaline explained that his father was an engineer at the college, and his mother was a pair of legals at the courthouse. He didn't mention about the condominium, because Mr. P. asked him if he had any brothers or sisters.

"Yes! As a matter of fact, I have two brothers who live in a tree house, along with their one hundred puppies and their motorcycle and their

Santiago Zeppelin, which is one of the fastest cars in the world."

Mr. P. clapped again, said, "Tell me all about them! Are these imaginary friends?"

Kaline felt a tug behind his ribs. But Mr. Putnaminski had said it with such excitement and understanding that Kaline felt like it was okay to say, "Yes, they're imaginary, which is as you know a very perfect kind of thing."

"Oh," Mr. P. said. "An imagination is a very perfect thing indeed."

Chapter Eleven

THE HOMECOMING

Kaline's DAD was allergic to dogs but Kaline's MOM was not, and so she and Mr. Putnaminski arranged for Maestro to spend ONE ENTIRE NIGHT A WEEK with Kaline, sleeping right on Kaline's bed with Banjo! It was the heavenliest time he had ever known. And every evening Mr. P. helped Kaline with his homework and IF IT COULD BE BELIEVED he knew more about history and math and reading and coloring than STEVE and NICKY COMBINED, although Kaline seriously doubted Mr. P. could dismantle a carburetor.

Kaline added Stumpy and Sandwich On A Stick to the village downtown, because who knew if they'd been there in 1945? The Stump probably had been, and if not that stump, then another. It turned out carving a stump out of balsa wood wasn't as easy as it sounded, but once Mr. P. had planted it in the woods behind his very own farmhouse, it looked EXACTLY and Kaline meant EXACTLY like a real stump.

After homework they walked Maestro, tickety tickety tickety down the street, and Mr. P. told him stories, about how one time he had wandered into a saloon somewhere deep in New Mexico, and it was just a very small single room and hanging above the bar was the shell of a giant turtle, a turtle nearly the size of the car! And when Mr. P. asked about it, the Indian woman who owned the bar told him the shell was all that was left after the nuclear testing at Los Alamos.

"Excuse me?" Kaline said.

"In the desert outside Los Alamos, New Mexico, where the United States tested the first nuclear bombs. Who would have thought there would be gigantic land turtles out there? Anyway, I sat beneath its shell and enjoyed a draft beer. The barkeep, as fine a woman as she was, had no teeth."

"ARE YOU SAYING THE TURTLE SHELL WAS RADIOACTIVE?"

Mr. P. shrugged. "Probably."

They talked about many things and then Kaline brought up that it was Friday evening and his dad would be coming soon to pick him up for the first time, for a visit to the condominium where he'd made a bedroom for Kaline. He couldn't WAIT to see his dad's car pull into the driveway—pull in PERFECTLY STRAIGHT, as he did. Even if Kaline got into the car and his dad complained about the yard or Kaline's shoes or Kaline's haircut or sitting up straight or move the table or keep your something-or-other at a right angle to something else or I will become physically ill—even if that's how it went, Kaline STILL couldn't wait. He was about to say those things to Mr. Osiris when here the car came down the street, dark blue and not a smudge on it, and it pulled into the driveway PER-FECTLY STRAIGHT. Kaline stood frozen, so Mr. Osiris gently pushed him toward his own yard.

Kaline's dad jumped out of the car, and there was his FACE! And his hair cut so perfectly his mother said it had to be done by scientists! In his worry Kaline shouted, "I'M SORRY ABOUT THE DO NOT WALK ON GRASS SIGNS, I TRIED, AND I'M SORRY I'VE BEEN WALKING ON THE GRASS AND ALSO MANY THINGS IN THE HOUSE ARE CROOKED!"

His dad was smiling so bigly his eyes were filled with tears and he yelled back, "Kaline, my boy! I don't care about any of that, you can pull up the grass and dig a hole and then put the grass back down like a wig for all I care! Come give me a hug!"

Kaline Klattermaster took off running, running toward his dad who was *found*. He had a feeling like when he got EXACTLY what he wanted for Christmas and was so happy he about had to throw up. Then his dad was swinging him in the air and Kaline was thinking, *I wonder how he knew about the wig grass.* Later he would ask his dad if maybe, just MAYBE he was some kind of spy, because that would be PANGEMONIUM.